Kamik
Takes the Lead

Note to Readers:

For Inuktitut-language resources, including pronunciation assistance for Inuktitut terms found in this book, please visit inhabitmedia.com/inuitnipingit

Published by Inhabit Media Inc. · www.inhabitmedia.com

Inhabit Media Inc. (Iqaluit), P.O. Box 11125, Iqaluit, Nunavut, X0A 1H0
(Toronto), 191 Eglinton Avenue East, Suite 310, Toronto, Ontario, M4P 1K1

Editors: Neil Christopher and Kelly Ward
Art Director: Danny Christopher
Designer: Astrid Arijanto

This project was made possible in part by the Government of Canada.

We acknowledge the support of the Canada Council for the Arts for our publishing program.

ISBN: 978-1-77227-266-6

Printed in Canada

Library and Archives Canada Cataloguing in Publication

Title: Kamik takes the lead / adapted from the memories of Darryl Baker ; illustrated by Ali Hinch.
Names: Baker, Darryl, author. | Hinch, Ali, illustrator.
Description: Series statement: The Kamik series
Identifiers: Canadiana 20190166479 | ISBN 9781772272666 (softcover)
Classification: LCC PS8603.A4525 K36 2019 | DDC jC813/.6—dc23

Kamik
Takes the Lead

Adapted from the memories of **Darryl Baker** · Illustrated by **Ali Hinch**

Jake waited at the starting line, sitting on his qamutiik. His dogs
stood in front of him, yipping and barking, excited to start the race. On
either side of him were other mushers and their dog teams awaiting their
starting time. The crowd watching counted down, "Three, two, one!" and
then cheered as each team went sailing over the snow.

Jake knew there were three more teams to go before his name would be
called. This was his first race, and the first time Jake's dog Kamik would
be leading a team of dogs in a race around town against the other young
mushers.

Kamik was tethered at the front of the pack, eager to start pulling but never distracted by the other dogs who were jumping and barking around him.

Jake and Kamik had worked hard preparing for this race.

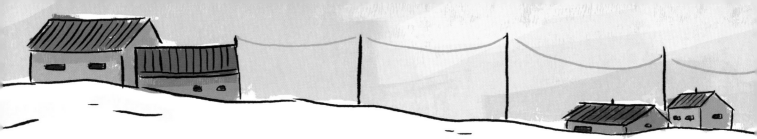

Almost a year earlier, Jake had asked his akkak, his uncle, if he thought Kamik was ready to start training for his first race. Kamik had run with his uncle's dogs a few times, and Jake felt ready to begin training a small dog team of his own.

"It will be a lot of work," Akkak said, "but if you are committed to training them, we can do it. It can take up to a year for dogs to be ready to run a race."

"I think I can do it," Jake said tentatively.

In the summer, when the weather was warm, Jake and his uncle took the dogs out on the land.

"Summer is the best time to exercise dogs. Running in the heat will make them very fit and strong," Akkak said.

Jake let his dogs run with his ATV. He made sure to give the dogs lots of rest and water.

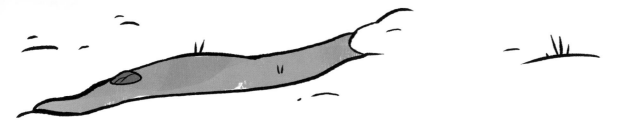

In the fall, Akkak showed Jake how to train the dogs with heavy sleds.

"In the fall, when it is cool, dogs can tend to run too fast, and they will tire out quickly," he told Jake. "A heavier load means that the dogs will trot instead of running full speed. That way they can practise running much longer distances."

Jake took his dogs out every day. Even days when he was tired and didn't feel much like training. Jake tried not to complain, because he knew training dogs was hard work.

"Dogs need to be taken care of all the time," Akkak told him. "You have no choice but to get the work done!" he said, giving Jake a pat on the back.

While they trained the dog team, Akkak was always watching Kamik to make sure that he had the qualities needed to be a good lead dog.

"Kamik is not easily distracted," he said with a smile. "He runs right to the end of his lead and keeps the lead tight. That is what you want to see in a lead dog."

Jake was proud of his team, and of Kamik especially.

Jake kept his team tied near a clean, fresh river where they would have lots of water to drink. His uncle taught him how to check that the dogs were healthy and well fed.

"I like to mix store-bought dog food with blubber or other country food and water," Akkak told him, "to make sure the dogs are healthy and get enough fat in their diet."

Jake spent lots of time with his dogs, even when they were not out training.

"Dogs have feelings, too," Akkak reminded him. "They need affection and care, and they can't be treated too harshly."

When wintertime came, Jake and his team were finally ready to run a farther distance from town.

Akkak helped him pack the sled with everything he might need if he were going on a long racing trip—tarps, a camp stove, food, a sleeping bag—everything! That way the dogs would get used to pulling a heavy load and would be able to run the distances needed to someday complete a very long race.

Before they left town, Akkak took him aside. "Remember," he said, "dogs can run very far in a short period of time. You can find yourself very far away from town if you are not careful. You should always have an adult follow you when you are training a dog team."

Jake listened carefully and promised not to take his team out on his own until he was older.

By early spring, the team was pulling well together. Kamik listened to Jake's commands and always did as he was told.

There was a community race in a few weeks, and Jake eagerly signed up to compete.

Jake and his uncle continued to get up early every morning to train his dogs. Jake rode on the sled while Akkak followed behind on his snowmobile.

The day before the race, Akkak brought him some fresh seal blubber to mix with the dogs' food. Jake fed his dogs and sat with them for a while, giving them some extra affection.

"We have our first race tomorrow," Jake said to Kamik. "Are you ready?"

Kamik wagged his tail and jumped to his feet. Jake smiled.

At the starting line, Jake heard the organizer call his name. It was his turn to run next!

He steadied himself on the qamutiik. He called to Kamik, who pulled his lead tight. Next to him in the crowd, Akkak gave him a nod. He was ready to go.

"Three, two, one!"

Jake started the team and felt the wind whip his cheeks as he and the dogs sped out across the bumpy snow.

Contributors

Darryl Baker is a teacher in Arviat, Nunavut. He was born in Churchill, Manitoba, and raised in Arviat. In 2006 Darryl graduated from the Nunavut Teacher Education Program, along with other Inuit from the same community, and he has been teaching at the Levi Angmak Elementary School since. Besides his career as a teacher, he enjoys dog mushing and has been an active participant in Hudson Bay Quest and other dog team races between Rankin and Arviat. He started raising dogs as a young man, picking up the interest from his late brother-in-law, Bernie Sulurayok. As a young boy, he often went hunting for seals at the floe edge with his brother-in-law. He eventually started raising dogs on his own, spending quality time with them and bonding strongly, gaining respect. Today he is still actively mushing and hopes to pass it on to his twin boys.

Ali Hinch has been working as a full-time illustrator and designer in educational kids' literature since getting her degree in illustration from Sheridan College. She's also dabbled in puppet concepts, set design, storyboarding, and writing for animation. Currently living in Toronto, she spends a lot of time drinking iced tea and making new dog friends.

INHABIT
MEDIA

Iqaluit · Toronto